LITTLE JASHANAFAR

MY FIRST ROSH HASHANAH

Book for Toddlers

Honey

About the Jewish New Year for Kids

PUBLISHED IN 2024 By Little Jashanafar

Rosh Hashanah
literally means "Head of the Year"

Rosh Hashana marks the moment
when we begin the Jewish New Year.

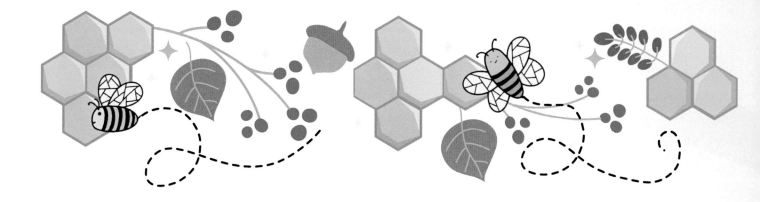

The Jewish year begins with *Tishrei*.
This month, Jews celebrate holidays that inspire
them to expect and pursue a better tomorrow.

Rosh Hashanah is one of Judaism's holiest days.

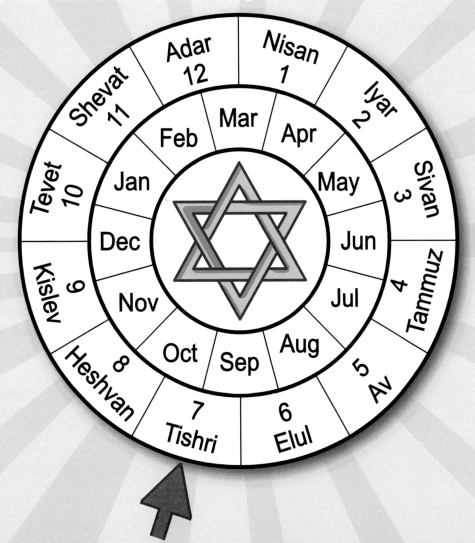

The holiday begins on the first day of *Tishrei*,
the seventh month of the Hebrew calendar,
which falls in September or October.

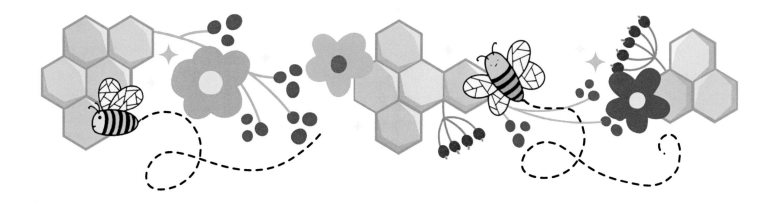

Rosh Hashanah has several names:

Yom Teruah

"The Day of Sounding (the Shofar)

Yom Hazikaron

"The Day of Remembering"

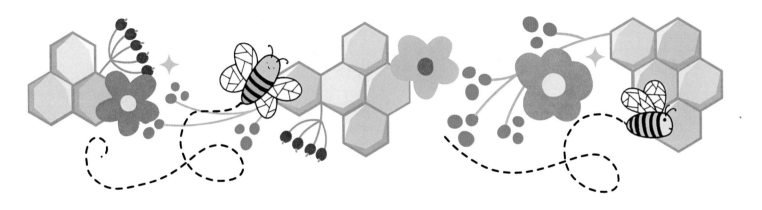

Yom Harat Olam
"The Birthday of the World"

Yom Hadin
"The Day of Judgment"

The Rosh Hashanah holiday is the anniversary of creation the first humans - Adam and Eve. On this day each year we begin a new cycle.

On this day **God** assigns blessings for the New Year.
The Book of Life is written
during the Rosh Hashanah holiday.
It writes in it our destiny for the coming year.
We pray that God will give us a fantastic one.

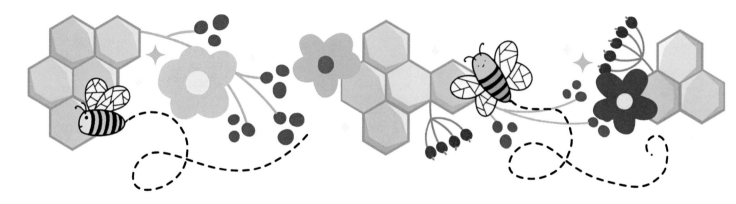

Another tradition of the Rosh Hashanah holiday is **Tashlich**.

Bread

This is a very important **ritual** involving the throwing of sins into water. The symbol of our sins are the bread crumbs that we throw into a pond, lake or river where there are fish, so feeding them.

During Rosh Hashanah we send cards to our family members to wish them Shanah Tovah, a Happy New Year!

SHOFAR

The Shofar is one of the most important symbols of Rosh Hashanah

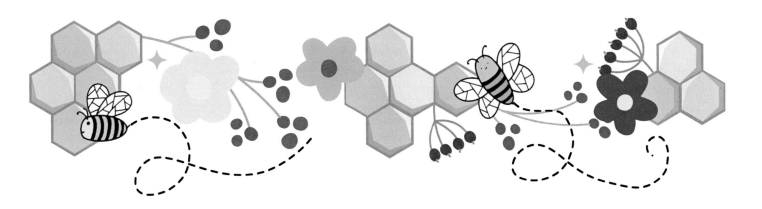

A Shofar is a trumpet made from a ram's horn.
This instrument is used
during Rosh Hashanah services.
The shofar makes a sound that calls for a return,
the sounds of the shofar are supposed
to awaken hearts and remind everyone
of what is good and right.

The shofar makes three types of sounds:
Tekiah, Shevarim and Teruah.

On Rosh Hashanah we dip pieces of apples in honey to symbolize our hope for a sweet new year. This is one of the traditions of this holiday.

Apples dipped in honey!

Rosh Hashanah is a sweet holiday,
it's a holiday of joy!

HONEY

Honey

Good & sweet New Year!

A hive is a home for bees

Bees are very hardworking.
They are the ones that produce sweet honey.

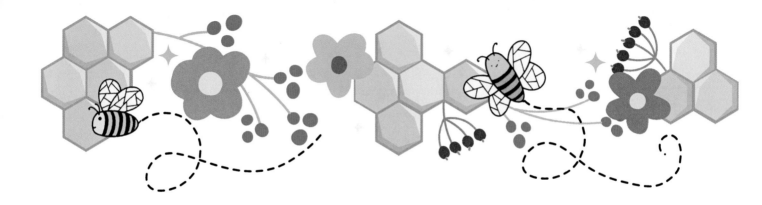

The pomegranate is one of the symbols of holiday.
It symbolizes the mitzvahs (commandments)
in the Torah, of that there are 613.
Eating a pomegranate and its seeds symbolizes
a wish for many good deeds in the coming year.

Celebrating new

POMEGRANATE
RIMON

Try to count all the pomegranate seeds!

Head of a Fish – „Head of the Year"

Fish

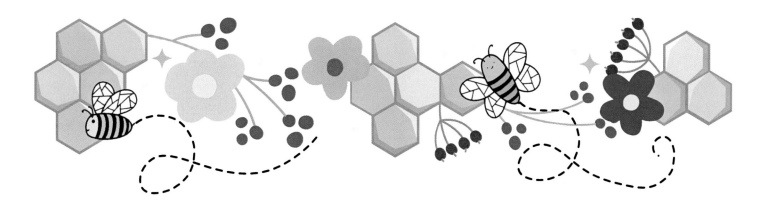

The fish's head is one of the most important
symbols of Rosh Hashanah.
Its role is to remind people that
they are **head** - leaders.

This symbol is supposed to remind people
to move forward, not to look back
and not to regret various things of the past.

ROUNDED CHALLAH

Challah during the Rosh Hashanah holiday is a **unique** one because it is **round** in shape and sweeter in taste.

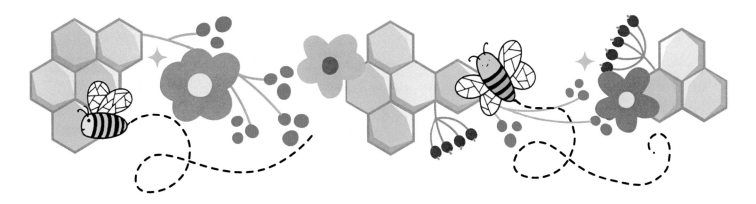

Challah is a very special Shabbat and holiday bread.

The round challah, which have no beginning
and no end, symbolizes the circular cycle of the year
and the never-ending cycle of Jewish life.

Rosh Hashanah Foods
that Jews eat for a Sweet New Year
- these are also symbols of this holiday!

By eating the pumpkin, we ask God to break all bad decrees against us and that our merits be declared before Him.

Pumpkin or gourd

Carrot symbolizes cancellation of negative decrees

Carrots

The leek is a symbol of concern to our enemies.
Eating leek symbolizes cutting off
(destroying)v enemies
so that they do not hurt us.

Leek

The **dates** symbolize the hope
that enemies will be overcome.

Dates

Leek and **dates** are eaten to protect us from enemies.

Beets are eaten to express hope that our enemies will leave.

Black-eyed peas

Beetroot

Jews eat **black-eyed peas** to symbolize all the good merits they should experience in the coming year.

During the Month of Tishrei, except for
Rosh Hashanah, we also celebrate the holidays:
Yom Kippur, Sukkot and Simchat Torah.

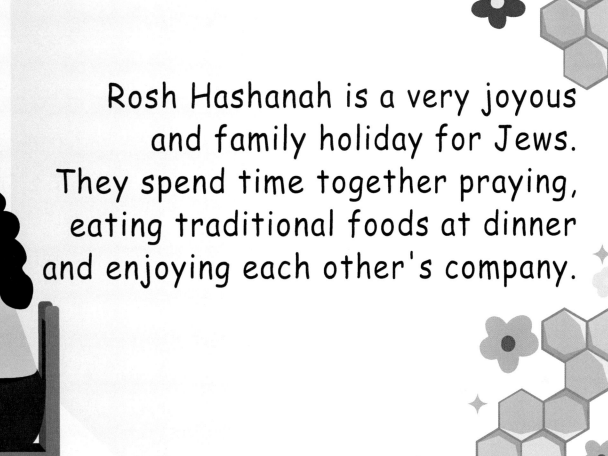

Rosh Hashanah is a very joyous and family holiday for Jews. They spend time together praying, eating traditional foods at dinner and enjoying each other's company.

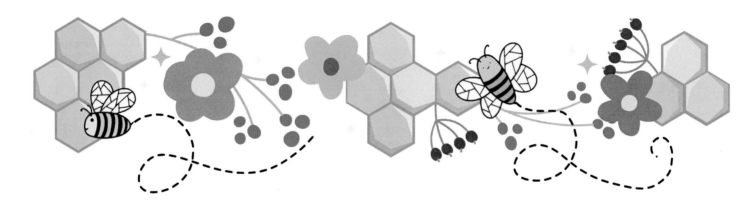

Rosh Hashanah lasts for two days.
It is an event in the Jewish calendar
that opens the period of atonement
that lasts until Yom Kippur.

Yom Kippur (Hebrew: "Day of Atonement")
marks the end of the Days of Atonement,
which comes 10 days after Rosh Hashanah.
Yom Kippur is the holiest day of Judaism.

Made in United States
Orlando, FL
29 September 2024